18262

Reuter, Margaret

My Mother is blind

DATE DUE

SEP 6 '80			
DEC 2 '80			

My Mother is Blind

Words by Margaret Reuter

Pictures by Philip Lanier

CHILDRENS PRESS, CHICAGO

3 4 5 6 7 8 9 10 11 12 R 85 84 83 82 81 80 79

Library of Congress Cataloging in Publication Data

Reuter, Margaret.
  My mother is blind.

  SUMMARY: A young boy describes how everyone
in his family comes to terms with his mother's
blindness.
  [1. Blind—Fiction. 2. Physically handicapped
—Fiction. 3. Mothers—Fiction] I. Lanier,
Philip. II. Title.
PZ7.R327My   [Fic]   78-12645
ISBN 0-516-02021-8

My Mother Is Blind

We are going to the park for a picnic today. We can walk all the way. I am carrying our lunch. Dad has the lemonade. His right arm is bent for Mother to hold. She can tell by the way he moves where to step. But she can't see anything. She is blind.

When my mother first became blind, she was very sad. She didn't want to do anything. She just sat in a chair and listened to the radio. Dad cooked and I washed the dishes. Dad told me I'd have to dust and pick up things I used to just leave around the house. I wanted to go out and ride my bike. But Dad said I'd have to stay home and help Mother all the time. That was before Mr. Green started coming to our house.

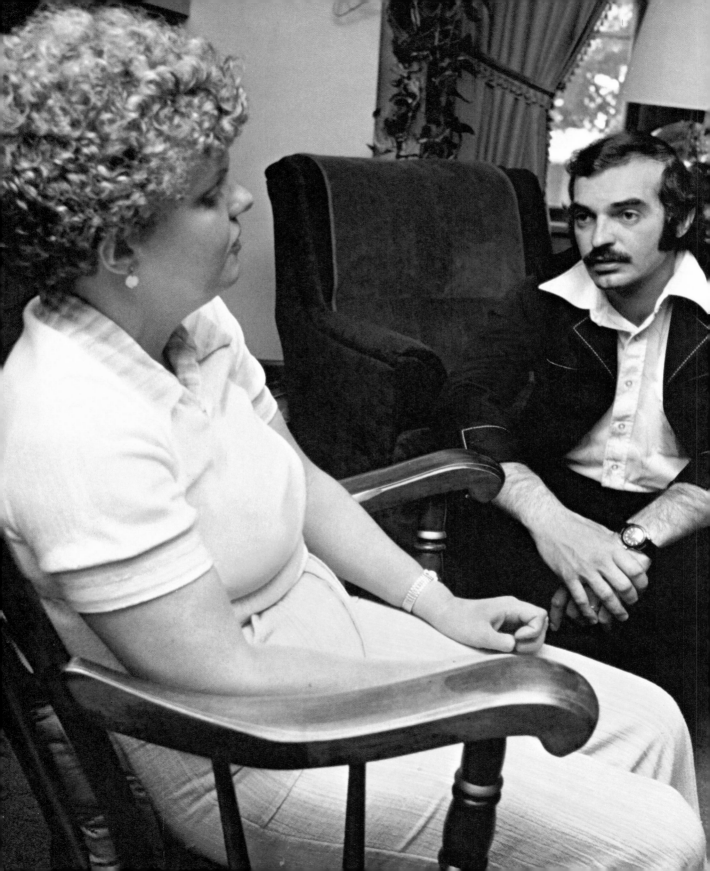

Mr. Green is a special teacher who finds ways to help people who can't see. He found out my mother really wanted to take care of Dad and me. She thought it wasn't safe for her to cook. She didn't know how she could clean the house when she couldn't see the dirt. She was afraid to walk alone because she might bump into things or fall.

I'm glad my mother learned to cook again. She made the cupcakes for our picnic. The directions are on a tape. She listens and then gets out the things she needs. She knows where to find everything. The different sized cups are in a certain place. So is the wooden spoon. The tape tells how to mix everything. Mother can tell when the cupcakes are done by the smell and the way they feel when she touches one with her finger.

Mother has learned to move around our house even though she can't see. She remembers where things are placed and how far it is to doorways. Mr. Green or Dad walked with her at first when she went outside. Now she has a long cane. It is a special stick that she moves from side to side as she walks. She can tell if anything is in the way. She can tell when the sidewalk ends or when there are steps. But she still likes it better when someone walks with her.

Sometimes I go to the store with Mother. I help her find the right cans and boxes. I hold the front of the cart and she pushes. When we get to the fruits and vegetables, I put her hand on the ones she wants to buy. She can tell by feeling and smelling when something is ripe or when it isn't fresh.

When it's time to pay, Mother gets the money out. She has a way to tell a dollar bill from a five-dollar bill. She keeps a paper clip on the five-dollar bills. She can tell a dime from a penny because the edge of the dime feels different. It has little ridges. She can tell the other coins by their size.

Mother wanted to be able to read, so Mr. Green began to teach her Braille. The word Braille sounds like mail. It is the way blind people read with their fingers. Braille books have dots that stick up above the paper. When you know what the dots mean you can read words. Now Mother's fingers move fast from side to side, touching the dots. She reads the words with her fingers and tells me the story. I look at the pictures and tell her what the colors are.

My mother can write Braille too. She puts a piece of paper between two plates. The top plate has openings like little windows. She uses a tool called a stylus to poke dots in the openings. Each opening can hold a Braille letter. The letters have to be made backwards. That's because you turn the paper over to read the dots. My mother puts Braille words on cans and jars and boxes. Then she can read what is inside.

My mother listens carefully. She can tell whether footsteps are coming or going. She knows people by their voices. She can tell from the sound of a car how close it is, what direction it is moving, and when it is stopping or starting. She always seems to know what I'm doing at home. When my friends and I play, we make a lot of noise. But Mother doesn't mind.

There's another way my mother listens.
When we walk down the street, she can tell
when she is close to a tree or a pole or a
building. She says there is a different sound
when something is there. I close my eyes and
try to do that, but I can't. I guess it takes a lot
of practice.

"Something smells very nice," my mother says. We are close to the park now. There are flowers along the path. Mother knows what kind they are. She remembers how different flowers smell. She takes care of our garden. She can even tell the weeds from the flowers. She knows the shapes of leaves. She feels them to tell one from another.

We have found a good place to have our lunch. Dad puts Mother's hand on the edge of a picnic table. She can find the bench by herself and sit down. I'm ready for some lemonade.

I know my mother can hear the sound of ice when Dad pours the lemonade. She can feel the cold and wetness on her glass. She can taste it when she drinks, sour and sweet at the same time.

I wish she could see.